Crow Girl Rises

by

Kate Cann

To the old man in the park

Visit Kate's website at –
www.katecann.com

First published in 2006 in Great Britain by
Barrington Stoke Ltd
18 Walker Street, Edinburgh, EH3 7LP

www.barringtonstoke.co.uk

This edition first published 2012

ISBN: 978-1-84299-993-6

Printed in China by Leo

Contents

Chapter 1
The Upper Hand

It was three days after Halloween. Crow Girl went into school with her head up and a big smile on her face. Three short days ago, Crow Girl hadn't existed. Three days ago, there had only been timid Lily Stanfield, the one who the vile Parkway Girls loved to bully.

But on Halloween night Lily had called up all her courage and turned up at Kyle Hooper's Halloween party. She wore the huge black wings she'd spent hours making. The crows she'd tamed in the woods flew around her head. Everyone was terrified – and then they saw it was Lily. She was the dark queen of the party after that. And now everyone – most of all, best of all, Kyle Hooper! – wanted to know how she'd done it. But so far only her friend Marsha was in on the secret.

From now on – Lily *was* Crow Girl! She'd been Crow Girl again last night. The Parkway Girls, angry at the way Lily had been the star of the Halloween party, had gone for her. But Lily and the crows had scared them off.

Now Lily needed Marsha's help. She spotted Marsha standing by the Science Block, and hurried over to her.

"Hi!" Marsha called out. "I talked to Miss Harland, about you helping with the costumes for the play!"

"Marsha, I've got to talk to you!" said Lily.

"I told her all about your brilliant wings," Marsha went on. "She wants you to come and see her – "

"Sure," said Lily. "Marsha, I – "

"Basically, there's two sorts of mutants in the play – the bird-people, and the sexy mermaids – I'm playing one of those."

"*Marsha!!*"

"What?"

"Listen to me!" begged Lily. "The Parkway Girls followed me last night!"

"Oh my God! Did they get you?" Marsha asked.

"No. I led them into the woods, and set my crows on 'em!"

"Wha–at?"

"It's true," Lily went on. "It was like at the Halloween party, only this time there were masses of crows. God, it was brilliant, Marsha! I made out I was throwing food, and the crows *covered* them! The Girls nearly passed out with fear – they just ran and ran, right out of the woods – "

"Oh my *God*! Excellent!"

" – The problem is, this morning the Girls'll be spitting mad, and I gotta keep the upper hand now. I need your help to – " Lily broke off. Marsha's face had changed – her eyes were huge and warning.

And then Lily heard: "Hi, *Crow* Girl!"

She spun round. All four Parkway Girls were standing there, with Tanya out in front. They were all glaring at her, mean and hostile, out for revenge. Something deep inside Lily told her that it all depended on how she acted now. She made herself look right back at them, made herself look into their eyes, forced her voice to be steady.

"Hey – nasty scratches on your arm, Jade!" she cooed. "Did something *attack* you?"

"Don't be stupid!" snapped Jade. "I did this on the bushes!"

"What – all *this*?" Lily reached out and grabbed hold of Jade's arm. Jade was furious. She pulled her arm away.

Lily laughed. She'd begun to feel a wonderful sense of power throbbing inside her. "How did you manage to tear yourself up that bad?" she said with a nasty smile.

"You better shut up!" squawked Jade.

"You must have been running *really* hard!" Lily went on. "And not looking where you were going! Hey – did something *scare* you?"

"You better shut up *now*, freak!" snarled Tanya. She took a step forward. "We think you're *sick*, and we don't like sick people!"

"You needn't think you're gonna get away with what you did!" Jade added, with menace in her voice.

"But what did I *do*?" mocked Lily. And she lifted both arms, as if she didn't know what they were talking about. But lifting her arms was her signal to the crows. And she knew the Parkway Girls would know that.

The Girls stepped back. They were scared. Tanya, furious, yelled, "*Don't* you try and pull that on us again! You might be able to stir up those filthy birds in the woods, but *they're* not here now, are they?"

"No!" sneered Jade. "They're not here now!" The Parkway Girls began to crowd forward again. Their faces came close up to Lily. She could feel their breath on her face, hostile and angry.

Lily made herself stand firm. She didn't back away. Instead she said sweetly, "No, I have to *call* them. Remember? But once I've called them, they'll follow me ... *ooh*, anywhere." She turned to Jenny, the quietest of the Parkway Girls, and stared at her intently. "Your house is near the woods, isn't it?"

There was a silence, just the sound of furious breathing. Then Lily said, "You should get those scratches seen to, Jade. Before they get infected."

And she walked calmly away.

Chapter 2
Payback?

"Yessss! *Yesssss!*" Inside the Year Ten Girls' toilets, Lily was punching the air like a footballer who'd just got a brilliant goal. Marsha was dancing round her, squawking, "That was amazing! I mean – just truly amazing! They were so *scared* of you!"

"You bet they were scared of me! They think I can set my crows on 'em, any time I want!"

"God, it was brilliant! Lily, you're my new hero! You took on all *four* of them! They backed off, it was fantastic ... in the old days,

7

they'd've grabbed you by the hair or something, but they didn't *touch* you ..."

Lily spun round and got hold of Marsha by both hands. "You know the best bit? I wasn't scared of them! I mean – I was at first, I was wetting myself I was so scared, but when I saw how nervous *they* were, it was just like – I was on a roll!"

Marsha hugged her, laughing. Lily laughed too, then she said, "OK, we've got to think. This is just the start."

"The *start* – ?"

"They're gonna come back at me, aren't they? They're not going to let themselves be shamed like that, not by *me*."

Marsha went over to the wash basins, and stood looking at herself in one of the mirrors above them. "I dunno," she said. "I haven't thought that far."

"Well, I've had overnight to think. Tanya's *not* going to let it lie. Not *now* – now it's two-nil to Crow Girl."

"So what are we going to do?"

"I've got to hit back again. I've got to hit back and scare them so they *stay* away – they gotta leave me alone for good. That was what I wanted to talk to you about. I need your help. I dunno how to do that."

There was a silence. Marsha stared into the mirror, and flicked her hair about. Then she said, "You know what you said about Jenny living near the woods and everything? You can't *really* get the crows after her, can you?"

Lily grinned. "Well, I could! But not as easily as I made out. I'd have to get them over to Jenny's house, tempt them with food and chuck a load of bacon rinds at her. Then ..."

"So what'll the Parkway Girls do? ... I mean, when they find out you can't just call the crows whenever you want to ..."

"Well ... I'm not going to let them find out! Look, we've both seen a load of films where people have some kind of supernatural power and go and kick ass, haven't we? They do the things *they* wanna do. The power works for them, right?"

"You mean like Spiderman?"

9

"Yeah. Or more like – where that girl finds out she's a witch."

"Right. I love that kind of film!"

"Good. 'Cos you're gonna help me make the Parkway Girls think they're *in* one! There's only one small hitch …"

"You've got no *real* power?"

"No real *supernatural* power. But I have got power, for sure. Power over their minds."

"*Mind* power."

"Yes. You saw how nervous they were, near me. You saw how it worked – I acted scary, like I had power, and they got scared. They think I'm weird, a freak. So – I'm gonna use that to play with. I'm gonna play with *them*. Stare at them, follow them, come round corners at them and make them jump …"

"That won't be enough."

"No. We need other stuff. I haven't worked everything out yet. I just know I've gotta scare them silly. Hey, come on, Marsha, don't look so worried! You're the drama queen! Are you in? I'm talking drama, here! Like what I did on

Halloween night! Magic shows and mind games!"

Marsha grinned. "You've really changed, you know that?"

"Have I? Good! Are you in?"

"Give me my orders, Crow Girl!"

Chapter 3
The Box

That afternoon, Lily and Marsha had science with two of the Parkway Girls, Jenny and Bella. Lily always kept well away from those two. Jenny and Bella might be weak but they were spiteful. They'd often try and pick a fight because they knew they had the power of Tanya and the rest to support them. But today, when Mr Roberts told everyone to get into fours to carry out an experiment, Lily gave Marsha a nudge. Then she walked over to Jenny and Bella's table. "OK if we two pair up with you two?" she asked, sweetly.

"No, it isn't!" snapped Jenny.

"Oh, come on," said Lily, firmly. She pulled out a chair and sat down at their table. "I want us to be friends again! After everything that happened yesterday!"

"Piss off, you mad bitch!" Bella hissed – just as Mr Roberts came up to the table.

"*Problems*, girls?" he barked.

"We don't want those two working with us!" snarled Bella.

"No, we *don't*!" squawked Jenny.

"Oh really?" said Mr Roberts. He sounded tired. "Given what everyone thinks of you two, I should think you'd be very grateful that *anyone* wanted to work with you! Now – get on with your work!"

As they got the experiment together, Marsha was over-helpful. She was *very* careful that no acids got splashed on the scratches on Jenny or Bella's arms. As Marsha fussed, Lily stared and smiled and stared at them until Jenny cracked. She screamed, "You better stop it, OK!"

"Girls," said Mr Roberts. *"Please."*

Just before the end of the lesson, while Mr Roberts was busy trying to get everything finished on time and the noise level was loud, Marsha slipped out of the classroom.

She came back in a few minutes later with an empty cardboard computer box. Marsha carried it very carefully, as if it was heavy or awkward. She put it gently on the floor beside her chair. Then she sat down and smiled.

"What's that?" snarled Bella.

"A box," said Marsha, sweetly.

"What's *in* it, idiot?"

"Oh – nothing for you to worry about." Marsha picked up her pen and started to write in her notebook. Then, from under the table by Marsha's feet, came a faint but definite scratching. It stopped for a few seconds, then it started up again, more loudly this time.

"What's *that*?" demanded Bella. "That noise?"

"What noise?" asked Marsha. She made a big deal of trying to listen. "There isn't any noise, Bella! You're imagining things!"

"No, I'm not, *bitch*! Can you hear it, Jenny?"

Jenny put her head on one side to listen, but the scratching had stopped. The girls settled back to their work – then it began again. *"There it is!"* yelped Bella. "It's coming from the *box*!"

"Oh, for *goodness* sake, what's got into you?" Marsha said. She sounded like a kind aunt who was getting tired of the children she was looking after. "You're really on edge today, aren't you? What's up?"

By now, Lily knew what Marsha was up to. She leant across the table towards Bella and said softly, "You do seem nervous, Bella. And you don't look that well, either. You're really pale."

"You need a good night's sleep," added Marsha. "Without any *bad dreams*." The scratching got louder still. Marsha bent down towards the box and whispered, *"Shhh ... shhhh!"*

"You're *sick*, you two!" Jenny said. Her voice trembled.

Lily bent down towards the box too. "Is he OK?" she murmured.

"Fine," Marsha murmured back. "He's fine!"

"You haven't got anything in that box!" said Bella in a shrill voice.

"Oh, really?" hissed Marsha. "Do you want to see?" She picked up the box, smiling nastily. The box looked as if it was moving. It was bucking and shifting about in Marsha's hands. Bella and Jenny stared at it, faces tight with fear.

"He really wants to stretch his wings, doesn't he?" Lily said.

Just then, the end-of-lesson bell blared out. Marsha shot to her feet and pushed the box across the table and straight at Bella's face.

"*Get that away!*" yelled Bella. She lurched backwards.

Marsha yanked the lid wide open. Something black was inside.

Bella screamed. She put her hands over her face, scrambled to her feet and pelted straight out of the classroom. Jenny was right behind her, just as terrified.

Mr Roberts looked up and saw the door bang behind them. "Any problems, girls?" he called out.

"No, sir!" trilled Marsha. "Bella just felt a bit sick, that's all!"

****

Lily and Marsha almost danced out of school that day. "Give that girl an Oscar!" gloated Lily. "You deserve it, Marsha! God, that was so *brilliant*! You're an ace actress! The way you held that box ... Even *I* thought a crow was gonna fly out of it!"

"Wasn't it *excellent*?" agreed Marsha. "I spotted the box by the bin, as we were going into class. All the time we were winding Jenny and Bella up, I was thinking what I'd do ... Then, when I nipped out to get the box, I found some black paper in the bin, so I crumpled it up and shoved it inside ..."

"What about that scratching?"

Marsha pointed at her feet. "My boot buckle. I undid it specially. I was rubbing it on the box. Good, eh?"

"Brilliant! It went like a dream, and we didn't even plan it!"

"But you caught on fast too, Lily," Marsha laughed. "You were great. God – they were *terrified* – "

"Well, they were still in shock from the crow-attack yesterday. I bet Bella's gonna say she really did see a crow in that box ... they'll be seeing crows everywhere now!"

"Did you see the way Bella was waving her hands about?" giggled Marsha. "She probably thinks the crow *flew* at her – !"

The two girls walked on, arm in arm. They felt so good. "So! *Three-nil* to Crow Girl and her trusty side-kick Marsha!" said Marsha. "You know – if it all goes like this, it's gonna be easy!"

"But we gotta keep coming up with different things, OK?" insisted Lily. "We gotta keep coming at them from places they don't expect – all the time!"

"Definitely. Keep at them 'til they give up and leave us alone – "

"– and everyone else. They gotta stop bullying and become nice people."

"Don't ask for the impossible, Lily! Hasn't this been a perfect day?"

"Perfect," agreed Lily.

But there was one thing which hadn't been perfect. All day long she'd wanted to bump into Kyle Hooper, but she hadn't even seen him. *That*, she thought, *is the problem when you go to a school as big as a shopping centre.*

Chapter 4
Feathers

Lily told Marsha she was going home the long way. She said goodbye, and set off on the lane that took her past the Wakeless Woods where the crows lived. Inside her bag was a fat tinfoil packet of crow scraps. She wanted to give the crows a reward for scaring off the Parkway Girls the evening before.

It was wet and dark on the narrow path through the woods. The leaves had fallen off the trees and the branches were black and dripping. Lily felt disappointed that the crows didn't come out to meet her. She got all the way to the oval clearing right in the middle of the woods before she saw them. The crows were roosting on the tree branches and they looked damp and miserable. "Hey," she called, "no sulking! I told you I'd make it up to you!"

The crows shifted in the trees. They turned their heads and peered round, then one by one they left their branches and flapped towards Lily.

"Look what I've got!" she cried. She started to throw great handfuls of scraps onto the ground. She watched happily as they stabbed at the food, picked up choice bits and flew off to eat on a branch in peace. Lily loved the crows' cruel, strong beaks that were never turned against her, and she loved the way they flew. They'd hop about as if they were witches on brooms, then they'd take off, strong wings flapping. It looked as if they had to work hard to keep from falling down. Lily liked that – she felt it was true to life!

A fight broke out between the Morrigan, the largest and greediest of the crows, and two of the others. The Morrigan was trying to chase them away from the scraps Lily'd brought.

"Stop it!" shouted Lily. "There's enough for all of you!" She threw another handful of scraps down, and the fighting stopped. A few black feathers had come out while they'd fought. Lily stooped down and picked them up. They were so glossy! She smoothed them out with her fingers.

Then she smiled. She'd had an idea.

She looked at the ground all around, and spotted three more feathers, which she picked up. Then she tipped out the rest of the food and called out to the crows, "OK, I'm going now. See you soon!"

White-flash flapped behind her as she made her way along the tiny, overgrown path. Then the crow overtook her and perched on a branch up ahead, waiting for her to catch up. She tossed it a few tidbits she'd kept back, but she wasn't really looking at it. She wanted to find more black feathers. She picked up another five. Then she came across a stunted bush with witchy-looking seed-pods on gnarled, twisted twigs. Lily broke off some of these, and put them in her bag. Then she hurried on out of the woods.

It was weird walking back along the lane. She had to walk right past Kyle's garden, past the same gate she'd gone through when Crow Girl was born, only a few nights before. She slowed down and enjoyed the memory of having all those eyes on her. She remembered the feeling of her wonderful wings lifting up and opening wide, how powerful she'd been ...

Suddenly, the door at the back of Kyle's house opened and someone stepped out onto the terrace. Head down, Lily fled. It could've been Kyle. What if he'd seen her hanging round his garden gate like some kind of stalker!

Chapter 5
Curse Charms

"Mum! You got any red thread?"

"What sort of thread?"

"It's gotta be strong. And real red – blood red!"

Lily's mum pointed to her sewing basket under the bench by the back door. "Have a hunt in there. I'm pretty sure I've got some."

"Thanks, Mum. I'm *starving*, by the way."

"Dinner in 20 minutes!" Lily's mum was smiling as she turned back to the spaghetti sauce that was bubbling on the stove. She still couldn't believe the way her daughter had changed. *Come out of her shell*, as she called it. Over the last few weeks, Lily had got more energy, she was walking tall, not slumping, and she was looking better all the time. She was trying out new make-up too. That was a bit, well, *weird*, but it did suit her. Her dark-dyed hair suited her, too. And best of all, since the weekend Lily was almost *glowing* with happiness …

"I'll be late home tomorrow, Mum," Lily said. "They've asked me to help out with costumes for the school play."

"Lily, that's wonderful! You've always been creative, ever since you were a little girl."

Lily tipped the crow feathers and gnarled twigs onto the table and her mum said, "Er … what are you *creating* now?"

"Oh, just something for the play," Lily said in an airy, don't-care way. She didn't think her mum needed to know that she was making curse charms to terrify the Parkway Girls!

She picked out four of the most twisted twigs. Then she tied two or three crow feathers onto each twig with the thick red thread. Some of the feathers dangled down, some stuck out at weird angles. Then as a finishing touch, Lily wound the thread round the witchy-looking seed-pods, and fixed a long loop at the top. "They look really nasty!" her mum said. "What exactly is this play about?"

Up in her bedroom, Lily sat in front of her mirror. She started to practise chilling and sinister smiles. She'd seen a horror film once with an evil doll in it. The doll had a horrible, neat little scary smile. It seemed to say *I'm a good girl and also I'm going to kill you.*

Lily practised that smile in the mirror until she felt she'd got it spot on.

Tomorrow was Day Two of the battle against the Parkway Girls.

Bring it on!

****

"You gotta see this!" squawked Marsha. She'd been waiting for Lily to get to school.

"No – you wait till you see *these*! I made 'em last night," said Lily.

"Lily – I've got a picture of a *crow* to text to the Parkway Girls!"

"What? Show me!"

Proudly, Marsha took out her phone. She showed Lily a photo of a savage-looking crow's head, with a mean eye and fierce beak. "Oh, that's *excellent*," Lily breathed.

"Isn't it?"

"Send it to me, too. I want it as a background picture."

"Sure! Now – I've got hold of two of the Parkway Girls' numbers – d'you think that's enough?"

"Yes – they'll show each other."

"I'm gonna get my big brother to text them," said Marsha. "That way if they want to phone back, they'll get this *stranger* who won't know what they're on about."

"Brilliant. Is your brother OK about it?"

"I had to promise to iron four of his shirts. But it's worth it."

"Great. Get him to send it *now*, Marsha! I've got another little surprise for the Parkway Girls at the end of the day ..." Lily took out the bag with the four curse charms in it.

Chapter 6
Mutant Mermaids

For the rest of that day, Lily followed the Parkway Girls around. She liked it when there was only one or two of them together, because that way, they felt more nervous. At break, she hid in some trees near Bella and Jenny and made crow noises. She watched them as they scanned the trees in fear. Inside school, she waited for Jade and Tanya round a corner and then peered at them with her evil-doll smile. She stared at them in class, eyes not blinking. When she saw Tanya show Jade the crow picture on her phone, she walked past them, smiling to herself. And she came close up

behind Bella and hissed, *"They're coming!"*
Bella nearly jumped out of her skin.

It was enormous fun. The Parkway Girls
kept telling her to clear off, that she was sick
and a freak. But they looked scared and, best
of all, they kept away.

At the end of the day, Marsha took her off
to meet Miss Harland the drama teacher. Lily
said, "You know something? I'm getting a bit
worried. I'm enjoying all this too much!"

"Why wouldn't you?" Marsha wanted to
know.

"I dunno. Maybe I'm becoming a bit of a
bully myself."

"Oh, *what?*" huffed Marsha. "You're not
bullying them, you're just warning them off.
When they've got the message that you don't
mess with Crow Girl ... we back off."

"Yeah, you're right. I'd be bullying them if
I *kept* going after them. If I didn't stop and
then got them *really* terrified."

There was a silence. Then Marsha gasped out, "That'd be quite good, actually, wouldn't it?"

"Brilliant! But we're not gonna sink to their level, Marsha – come on."

"No. I suppose not," said Marsha. "Shame."

****

The meeting with Miss Harland went very well. She told Lily she'd love to have her "on board" and she was really excited about the wings Marsha had told her about. She asked if Lily could bring the wings in to show her. Then she asked if Lily had any ideas about how to make the mutant mermaids' tails. Lily thought maybe they could dye old duvets sea-green and then cut and sew them up to look kind of odd and lumpy. She thought you could sew on milk bottle tops to be the scales. Miss Harland got so excited about this that Lily promised she'd show her some sketches by the end of that week.

As the girls were leaving the drama studio, Kyle Hooper walked in. "Hello, Crow Girl!" he grinned.

"Hello," Lily said, blood thumping. She'd seen him on and off, during the day, but they'd never had a chance to talk.

"Kyle!" Miss Harland called out. "Thanks for coming! Pete Tomms tells me you've agreed to help out with the lighting after all!"

After school, Marsha and Lily headed arm in arm out of the school gates. "Yes, it is!" Marsha insisted. "That's why Kyle wants to help out with the play. It *is* 'cos he wants to be near you! I know for a fact he said he wouldn't help, and now he says he will! What's changed? It's 'cos *you've* got involved!"

"It's called a *coincidence*, Marsha!" Lily said, but she felt so excited and happy she couldn't stop grinning.

"*Sure* it is! What about how he wouldn't leave you alone at his Halloween party, hmm? And I saw the way he looked at you in History, he's ..."

Marsha broke off, because Lily had stopped dead in her tracks. "Oh my God, all this talk about Kyle nearly made me forget!" she said. She handed Marsha her school bag, pulled out the curse charms, waved them at Marsha, and pelted back into school.

Chapter 7
Show Down

"Is this filth something to do with *you*?" spat Tanya. She chucked four red strings of twig and feathers and seed-pods down on the table in front of Lily and Marsha. It was break time the next morning. The four Parkway Girls had got together, got their courage up, and come looking for Lily.

"Oh my *Go … o … od* – you've touched them!" moaned Marsha. "It's really bad to … *touch them!*"

Lily looked over at her friend. Marsha was fantastic. How that girl could act!

"Of course I touched them!" snarled Tanya. "We wanted them off our lockers!"

"Your *lockers?*" echoed Marsha, her eyes huge. "How did they get *there?*"

"Oh, I'm gonna smack you one in a minute!"

"I wouldn't do that," hissed Lily. She glared back at Tanya. Then she smiled her best evil-doll smile.

"Look – you don't scare us with your voodoo crap," Tanya said. But her voice shook.

"Are you sure?"

"Look, all I know is, we get in this morning and these nasty pieces of shit are hanging off our locker handles."

"It was horrible – they looked so *evil!*" squeaked Jenny.

"But you've pulled them off, Tanya!" groaned Marsha, and she shook her head. "You *touched* them!"

"It *was* you, wasn't it?" Jade said. "These are *crow* feathers!"

"And was it you who sent that foul crow picture?" Bella went on. "On my mobile?"

"And mine!" spat Tanya. "How did you get my number?"

"Sick cow! Getting some guy to cover for you!" Bella hissed.

"You have got a *twisted* mind!" Jenny added.

Lily stared right back at them all, did her doll-smile and said calmly, "That's right. My mind is *very* twisted."

There was a long, long pause. The air seemed to shudder around them. Then suddenly Marsha collapsed forward onto the table. "Tanya – you touched *all* of them!" she moaned. "If you touch *all* of them, the curse on all of them goes *straight to you!*"

Tanya went a pale shade of green. "I've had enough of this!" she yapped. "I'm off!"

"Don't leave them here!" begged Marsha. "The only way to stop the curse – *especially now you've touched them!* – is to burn them! At midnight! Over a heap of pine cones!"

"*Rubbish!*" squawked Tanya. She turned and stamped off. The other three Parkway Girls followed her. Lily and Marsha watched them. They stopped just outside the class and started to talk together in scared, angry whispers.

Lily and Marsha strained their ears and tried not to explode with laughter. They heard one of the girls say: "They're *crow* feathers!" Then they heard, "If she can make crows attack people what else can she do?" Then, "It's all right for you," hissed Tanya, "I'm the one with all the *curses* on me!"

Then Bella came creeping back to the table with a plastic bag round her hand. She scooped up the curse charms and took them off with her. "Midnight, remember!" called out Marsha. "Over pine cones! And it's best if you starve for six hours first and do it ... *naked!*"

****

At lunch, Marsha and Lily were talking about their success and laughing again when Kyle walked by with a loaded tray. "Hey, anyone sitting here?" he asked.

"I'm just going!" squawked Marsha. She picked up her half-eaten burger and shot to her feet.

"Marsha ...!" pleaded Lily. She felt hot and embarrassed.

"See you, OK?" Marsha sang, and scooted off.

"Something I said?" shrugged Kyle. He sat down across from Lily. "So – how are you?"

"Fine!" squeaked Lily.

"So – are you still the Morrigan, crow goddess, bringer of doom and despair?"

"Not today."

"So don't tell me – now you're Crow Girl – Superhero!"

"That's right!" Lily laughed. "I turn into a crow, and fly around fighting evil – "

"No, not evil – *good*. If you were a crow, you'd fight good."

"Don't you diss crows! They're fantastic birds! They've got *style*."

38

"Oh, what? Tell me one thing about them that's got style."

"The way they look – the way they fly! And ... in the spring, they don't mess about with bits of sheep's wool and moss for their nests, they flap around with these serious bundles of sticks in their beaks ..."

Kyle grinned. "Crows are *nasty*. Pecking out eyeballs, feasting on rotting rabbits and stuff ..."

"They're not!" Lily leaned over and pinched one of Kyle's chips. "They're fantastic, they're intelligent, and loyal ..."

There was a pause. Both of them smiled. Then Kyle said, "Those crows, flying round you when you turned up at my party. They were real, weren't they?"

Lily took in a breath. "Yes," she said.

"Not some kind of magician's trick, like people said – or from a projector or something?"

"No."

"I wanna see them."

"OK. You can."

"Soon?"

"Soon."

Chapter 8
Kyle in the Woods

"How much further?" grumbled Kyle, half-joking. "You just want to get me into these woods to give me a good snog, don't you?"

"You should be so lucky," Lily laughed back.

It was one week later, and Kyle and Lily had spent a lot of time together. They'd got a lot, lot closer.

Close enough to stand so near together behind the stage at the play rehearsal that they were almost kissing.

41

Close enough for Kyle to lean across the table at lunch and ask Lily to go out with him that weekend – a film, and then Pizza Express maybe.

Close enough for Lily to invite Kyle to come and meet her crows at last.

"I'm getting scared," said Kyle. "It's all gloomy in these woods."

"Take my hand then, baby boy."

They held hands and walked on, pressing close to each other. In her other hand Lily had an enormous bag of scraps. She hadn't been to the wood for days. Somehow, there'd been so much else to do this week – and she meant to reward her darling crows properly. As well as to get them to put on a real show for Kyle, of course.

"What's going on with you and the Parkway Girls?" Kyle asked. "You got something on 'em?"

"What d'you mean?" asked Lily with a smirk.

"This morning, I heard them call you sicko. And psycho. But it was ... kind of under their breath. And when you walked towards them ... I dunno. They just backed off."

"Did they?" asked Lily. She felt even better. "Didn't notice."

She had noticed, of course. Noticed and enjoyed it all. She and Marsha had kept up their war with the Parkway Girls, but now they were starting to ease off a bit. Marsha reckoned they needed to get hold of a stuffed crow to pep things up again.

"Here we are," Lily said. They were at the oval clearing. She turned to look at Kyle, desperate for him to like it.

He smiled back, and said, "Neat. Where are they, then?"

Lily stepped into the middle of the clearing. She took in a breath, lifted her arms, and called, *Kaa-kaaa-kaaaa!*

Her crows clustered round on the branches above them, turning their heads towards her. She threw up a handful of food. The crows tumbled in the air, and caught it. "They're great!" Kyle whooped. "Wow, this is something else, Lily – *you're* something else!"

She tossed a biscuit down at Kyle's feet and he waited nervously as White-flash hopped towards him. White-flash's eyes were like pinpoints on either side of its big, black, Roman-Emperor beak. It grabbed the biscuit, then, when Lily called out, flew back to her again.

"God, they really love you, don't they?" Kyle said. "It's not just the food, is it?"

"I dunno. I hope not. I thought they might be pissed off at me, 'cos I haven't been for so long ..."

"Nah. Look at them, all watching you!"

Lily threw the last of the food on the ground and the crows gathered up three or four scraps at a time, then carried them back to the trees. "That's it," said Lily. "My bag's empty. Shall we go?"

"Not yet," said Kyle. He walked over to her, grinning, and put his arms round her. Then he ducked down and kissed her, straight on the mouth. Lily, heart thudding, craned up to him,

44

and kissed him back. Lily had never had a boyfriend, and she'd only kissed two other boys before this, and it hadn't worked, it hadn't felt right –

But this *worked*.

Kyle drew back. "Wow," he breathed. Then he moved in and kissed her again.

Behind them, on the trees where the crows roosted, there was a stirring, a shifting.

Kyle pulled Lily closer in towards him. "You're brilliant," he murmured. *"Different."*

White-flash left its branch, flapped down and hung hovering over their heads, but Lily was too caught up with Kyle to notice. "You too," she whispered back. They kissed again, stronger than before, folding into each other.

The crow Lily called the Morrigan left its branch and joined White-flash, then Ragwing.

"You're gonna come out with me, aren't you, Lily?" Kyle said. He stroked her hair back from her face.

"Yes," grinned Lily. "If you want me to."

One after the other, the crows were leaving the trees, and now there were seven slowly circling above the loving couple.

Kyle threw back his head and shouted, "I got Crow Girl for my girlfriend!" Then he put his arms around Lily, and swung her off her feet.

Lily could hardly follow what happened next. All she remembered afterwards was a harsh, screaming blur of black, wings like ragged cloth and claws like knives and jealous, cruel beaks, stabbing, stabbing ...

Just a beating blur of black, a screaming swirl of black, everything black, and then red, red, more and more and more *red* ...

Chapter 9
Scars

Mobbed was the word the doctor had used. Mobbed by crows. The doctor had heard of seagulls doing that to climbers on cliff faces. "The climbers get too near the nests, you see, and the gulls go in for the attack, great clouds of them. I heard of some crows who mobbed a dog once too. The dog got near their young ones ..."

The nurse had looked at him with a grim face. "It's November," she said. "No nests – no babies."

"Ah," said the doctor, "ah, you're right." He turned back to the two teenagers that the ambulance had brought in and who now sat side by side in silence.

An elderly dog walker had found them, in the woods. They'd both been in a state of shock. They hadn't been able to say what had happened to them, but luckily the dog walker had her mobile with her. She'd been able to get help fast.

"What I don't get," the nurse said, "is that most of the injury is to the lad, here. Look – his arms have been torn to ribbons, but the girl's arms have hardly a scratch on them."

"Maybe the boy was protecting her," said the doctor. "Being brave."

"Maybe," said the nurse.

****

Lily was told she could go home from hospital after only two hours. The doctor told her to rest. She spent the next day in bed, hunched up under her duvet. Then she went back to school. Her mother insisted that

48

brooding at home never did anyone any good. Lily'd had a shock but she wasn't hurt, not like poor Kyle. She needed to get back to her old routine.

The story of the crow attack had gone like lightning round the school. Lily was a kind of spooky celebrity now, she *was* Crow Girl. "You should see the way the Parkway Girls are looking at you," muttered Marsha, as they made their way into the canteen at lunchtime. "They look totally *awed*."

"Yeah?" mumbled Lily. She didn't care. She felt tired of everything.

"I know this doesn't help much, Lil, but we don't need to worry about stuffed crows and all that now. After this, I don't think they'd ever dare pick on you again!"

Lily didn't answer. Nothing made her feel better. She felt as if her life had turned against her, become her enemy. Nothing seemed to matter except for the fact that Kyle and the crows had been taken away from her.

But she knew Marsha was trying to cheer her up, so she tried to smile back at her.

****

Kyle was out of hospital in two days. The doctors had stitched his arms up and told him he'd have an amazing set of scars to show off, once the slashes on his arms healed. They told him the scratch near his left eye would look quite sexy, like a duelling scar. They told him he was lucky not to have lost the eye.

He was told to rest for at least a couple more days at home.

Marsha took it on herself to find all this out, then told Lily in a no-arguments voice that she had to go and visit him.

Chapter 10
Visiting Kyle

"I can't," sobbed Lily. "He'll slam the door in my face!"

"Look – Kyle knows it wasn't your fault! You didn't set them on him, did you?"

"No, but ... he'll have gone right off me."

"*Lily!* What d'you think he'll think of you, if he still likes you, and you *don't* visit him?"

Lily had no answer to that. So that evening, she went round to visit Kyle. She felt she needed even more courage to do this than she'd needed for Halloween night.

She put down a box of Quality Street next to him on the sofa and said, "That's to say sorry. I mean – I know it can't. A stupid box of sweets. But ..." And then she burst into tears.

Kyle was on his feet right away. He put a bandaged arm round her. "Hey, come on," he said. "It wasn't that bad."

"Yes, it was!" Lily sobbed. "And it was all my fault!"

"Don't be daft. It was ... what did that doctor call it? A freak of nature."

"It wasn't! It wasn't! You know it wasn't!"

"*I* know – ?"

"You said yourself how much they love me. I *trained* them. And then I don't visit them for a week ... and then when I *do* go, I've got you with me, and we're kissing ..."

"Lily," groaned Kyle. He held her tight.

He's just feeling sorry for me, Lily thought. I bet he wants me to go. His arms round her felt so good, she started crying again. "They wanted me for *themselves*!" she wailed.

Kyle wanted to say he didn't blame them. He wanted to say he liked her so much that even the crows couldn't put him off. But he couldn't think how to say all that. So what he did was kiss Lily, and it was just as good as the kiss in the woods – maybe better.

Lily was stunned. She felt like life was turning towards her again.

"Have you been back to see them?" he whispered.

"No," she muttered. Her mouth was very close to his. "I hate them, for what they did to you."

"No, you don't. I've been thinking – the crows were protecting you. They thought I was attacking you, and when I lifted you up like that ..."

"I don't care. I hate them."

"No, you don't. Come on, Lily – you're Crow Girl!"

Lily was laughing, then crying, then laughing. She could hardly believe what was happening. How could Kyle want to be with her still? And he was right, she didn't hate her crows, not deep down. She wanted to see them again, they'd made everything come right for her. But, *but* ... when she remembered the way they'd attacked Kyle, the fierce cloud of black and then the *red*, all that *red* ...

"Look," Kyle said, and held her close, "I don't ever want to see those murdering little bastards again. Not unless I've got an AK-47 machine gun on my shoulder. The very thought of them creeps me out. But – I dunno. They'd never hurt *you*. They hurt me 'cos they love you. And ... the way they brought us together and everything ... and the scars I'm gonna have ... well. I think it's freaky and everything, but ... *well*, I also think it's pretty cool."

"You are *joking*!" Lily gasped.

"Why am I joking? It's cool to have a girlfriend who has crows as pets and not a stupid hamster! Or a cat. Or a goldfish or something."

"Yeah?"

"Yeah! And another thing – Mike's got scars from being beaten up. Rory's got scars from coming off his bike. I got crow scars. I mean – come on! Which has more style? Crow scars! It's nearly as good as a shark bite."

Lily burst out laughing, and hugged him. "So you really think it's OK?" she asked. "*We're* OK?"

"Yes, I do. Yes, we are," said Kyle. "I still want to go out with you, Lily. Even though you're so *weird*!"

Lily couldn't say a word. She couldn't remember feeling this good, ever, not even on Halloween night.

"After all," Kyle went on, "we don't have to do everything together, do we? You don't have to share my football ..."

"And you don't have to share my crows!" Lily reached up, pulled his head down to hers, kissed him. "One thing, though," she murmured.

"What's that?"

"You'd better not cheat on me or – "

"I know, I know. Or you'll set your crows on me again!"

Chapter 11
Forgiveness

A few days later, Lily went back to the woods to feed her crows. She felt both scared and excited as she walked along the little overgrown path. She kept getting flashbacks to the crows attacking Kyle and although that was horrible, it didn't make her want to turn round. She was longing to see them again.

She reached the oval clearing and the crows all flew up in a noisy, frantic cloud, as if they hadn't expected her to come again. As she opened the bag of food, her hands were trembling. She threw great fistfuls on the ground, and they flapped down and feasted. Lily watched them. She smiled to herself.

Then she said, "*Right*! I've got something to say to you lot. My life is brilliant now. The Parkway Girls are scared of me and Marsha's my best mate and I like how I look and they love my costumes for the play and – Kyle is my boyfriend! *OK?* You didn't spoil it, and I've forgiven you for what you did – almost. But if you ever, *ever* do anything like that again, that's it! It's over! I'll never come and see you – ever again!"

The crows, stabbing around for the last of the food, didn't even look up.

"Are you listening?" Lily went on, in a firm voice. "From now on – you stay in the woods, OK? I'm grateful for the way you came to the Halloween party, and then how you chased off the Parkway Girls. But from now on – we meet here, and here alone, and I won't ever bring anyone to see you, ever again, OK?"

If crows could shrug, Lily felt, her crows would shrug now. She laughed, and tossed the last of the food to them. Then she set off down the path again. She couldn't help it, she still loved them. In a strange way, she thought she loved them even more now.

****

A few weeks later, Lily was perched on one of the benches by the sports field. She was excited. She'd come to watch Kyle play football. It was an important match against another local school. There were only a few minutes to go and Kyle's team was one goal ahead.

Things were going brilliantly between Kyle and Lily, and getting better all the time. Lily wrapped her arms round herself, hugging herself with how good she felt. She watched Kyle, rather than the game. She cheered him on as he made an excellent tackle. The Parkway Girls, passing by on the far side of the field, stood and looked at her for a moment. But when Lily looked up at them, they walked away.

The final whistle went and a massive roar went up from Kyle's team. Kyle came hurtling over and Lily sprang up and gave him a big kiss. Then he ran back to celebrate with his mates.

****

Later, when they were walking home with their arms around each other, Kyle said, "I saw the Parkway mob at the match. They kept well away from you."

"Yeah. I can't believe they're still leaving me alone. I stopped going after them with crow stuff ages ago."

"Well, Lil – you looked a bit like a crow on that bench. All hunched up in your black coat and all."

"Did I? Great!"

"Yeah. Sinister, but gorgeous."

"Or maybe it's you," Lily laughed. "Maybe they know you'll protect me if they start again."

Kyle rubbed his cheek against Lily's thick, glossy hair. "You just don't get it, do you?" he murmured.

"Get what?"

"It's not about the crows, it hasn't been for ages. And it's definitely not about me. It's *you*."

Lily pulled away from him a little, so she could see his face. "Me?" she echoed. "What d'you mean?"

"Lily, you're not the kind of girl who gets bullied any more. You haven't been for ages. You're too *strong* now, too happy. People like the Parkway Girls sniff out fear like dogs. And they don't smell anything on you now, so they keep away."

There was a pause, while Lily thought about what Kyle had said. "D'you really think that's true?"

"I don't think it – I *know* it. It's not the crows they're scared of, not any more. And I'm not just saying that 'cos I don't want to give those murdering little beaky bastards any credit. They helped you – but it was you who grew strong. No one's gonna bully you now."

Chapter 12
Crow Girl Returns

The school play was ten days before the end of the Christmas term. It was a huge success. Everyone said the acting and the costumes were superb. They thought the mutant mermaid tails were fantastic. When the play was over, Lily longed for the Christmas break. She wanted more time to spend with Kyle. The weather suddenly turned very cold, and everyone said it might be a white Christmas. Lily took the crows extra food. The frost had changed the Wakeless Woods into a magical, glittering cavern and Lily loved it.

Lily and Kyle always met now by the gate at the bottom of his garden, so they could walk to school together. This gate, which led onto the lane that ran alongside the Wakeless Woods, had become quite important to them. It was where Lily had made her first stunning entrance as Crow Girl, back on Halloween night. Nowadays, it was where they did a lot of kissing and cuddling when they said goodbye after school. Kyle would never agree to walk further into the woods with Lily. Lily totally understood. What if her crows attacked him again?

One morning Kyle met her there, and said, "Your little beaky bastards were right here at this gate yesterday evening! They were trashing a rubbish bag."

"What?"

"People all up the lane have been saying how it's not foxes to blame, it's crows! They tear the bin bags open for food!"

"Aw – the babes! They're hungry!"

"They're *messy*! I had to clean up after the little sods!"

Kyle was acting angry, but Lily knew he wasn't really. She got hold of his arm, pushed up his sleeve, and stroked the crow scars there. The scars were growing fainter every day. "You're great, you know that?" she laughed.

He laughed back, then put his arm round her and they started walking. "Christmas soon," he said. "You *wait* till you see what I've got you."

Sometimes Lily felt it was all too much, too perfect. She couldn't see how it could go on, being this perfect.

Later that morning, Anna Blake and Bryony Cooper, both from Year Seven, came running up behind Lily. "Can we speak to you a minute?" they called to her.

"Sure," she said. She turned round to meet them.

"We need your help!" Anna wailed.

"We're getting picked on by the Parkway Girls!" Bryony moaned.

The two Year Sevens told her how the Parkway Girls had followed them out of school, then they'd forced them to hand over their money. Lily felt more and more angry as she listened. "It was after band practice, on Tuesday," Bryony said, in a trembling voice. "They waited for us ... they said they're gonna wait for us every Tuesday from now on!"

"It's not just us, either," added Anna. "They got hold of Mira, and Steff ..."

"Christmas'll be ruined!" sobbed Bryony. "All Christmas – I'll be dreading coming back to school!"

Lily thought of the way she'd been too terrified to come back to school last summer, and something inside her exploded. "They're disgusting!" she spat. "You've got to tell your teacher!"

The girls' faces crumpled. "But ... we're telling *you*!" squeaked Bryony.

"You're *Crow Girl*!" Anna said.

Lily felt her heart sink. She took a deep breath and was about to say she wasn't *really* a witch or a superhero. All that had been tricks and mind-games, and then that awful "freak of nature" with Kyle. There really wasn't anything she could do ...

But something stopped her. Instead, she asked, "Where did they jump you?"

"On our way home," said Bryony. She still sounded scared.

"Show me where," Lily said.

The girls showed her an alley ten minutes' walk from school. It was near the lane that ran beside the Wakeless Woods. The alley had high walls, and where it met the road there was a patch of grass where three tall, skinny trees grew.

It was perfect.

She took a deep breath, and said, "OK, Anna, OK, Bryony. Leave it to me."

****

"You don't have to come near the crows," Lily said. She, Marsha and Kyle were walking into town together at lunch-time. "You just have to help out with the food."

66

"No problem, I'll help," said Kyle. "As long as I can wear thick gloves, safety goggles and carry a baseball bat."

"Oh, shut up! It was *you* who gave me the idea, when you said the crows had been ripping open all the rubbish bags along the lane! Listen – if I drop food all the way along the lane to the road I can train them really quickly. They're so *intelligent*."

"Here we go," Kyle said with a groan. "Crow worship time."

"And then – next Tuesday," Lily went on, "the day of the last band practice … I get the bravest of them to follow me to the alley …"

"And scare the crap out of the Parkway girls," Kyle said. "Brilliant!"

"What about your costume?" Marsha broke in. "You gotta wear your wings … or a cloak – a long, black cloak. And your hair … I see a kind of … evil, twisted tiara, or some kind of crown, maybe …"

"Let's not go over the top, Marsha!" laughed Lily. "I'll wear black, but I don't want to look like I'm in a pantomime. I just want to look – "

"Like you," said Kyle. "Like Crow Girl is ... *you*."

Chapter 13
The Alley

That evening, Lily put the first part of her plan into action. She met the crows at the edge of the Wakeless Woods and instead of going into the trees with them, she turned back onto the lane. The hungry crows cawed with anger until she tipped out some tasty looking scraps. The crows fell on the scraps greedily. Lily walked along the lane, stopping every now and then to tip out food and the crows followed her right to the edge of town. Then she turned back.

She did this the next day, and the day after that. Lily tipped the food out on the exact same places. All week she carried on and all over the weekend. Each time she walked a bit further into town. Marsha and Kyle asked their mates to get together big bags of tasty food scraps to help out. By Monday, Lily was sure the crows were ready.

She found Bryony and Anna, and told them Tuesday was Crow Day. As soon as the Parkway Girls came up, they were to run for the alley. The Parkway Girls would follow.

They were to stop in front of the three skinny trees, and then leave it all to her. She promised them that whatever happened, they wouldn't get hurt. Bryony and Anna, their eyes huge, agreed.

****

As soon as school was out on Tuesday, Lily and Kyle raced back to his house. She changed into a black top and black jeans, and borrowed his black leather jacket. Then she put on black eyeliner and lots of red lipstick. "Scary?" she asked.

"Sexy," he said.

"So come with me!"

"Not so sexy that I'd risk having my head torn off. I'll wait here, OK?"

Lily laughed, kissed him, and set out. She met the crows, a black, beating, cawing cloud of them, and headed towards town. She tipped out food onto all the places where she'd put food before, but only small amounts this time. She wanted her crows to be still hungry, and getting angry.

At the end of the lane, she stepped out onto the path, and to her relief the crows followed her. Every few steps she threw up a few scraps, and they kept coming. Lily couldn't believe her luck. She was expecting half of them to turn and flap back to the safety of the woods, but they kept coming.

Lily got to the alley, and turned to go down it. At least ten crows were flying round her. She threw up one last fistful of food, and they swooped and fought over it. Then she hid behind one of the skinny trees and put the food bag on the ground. She stood very, very still.

At first, the crows flustered and cawed loudly, then one by one, they landed on the bare branches of the three trees. The trees looked as if they'd suddenly grown a mass of enormous black pine cones.

Lily could barely breathe, it was so perfect. She stood there, willing Bryony and Anna to be the next people into the alley.

Then she heard them. First, the sound of running, then Tanya shouting, "Come on, you stinking kids, pay your taxes!" and Jade squawking, "Pay up or get mashed!" Bryony and Anna skidded into the alley and, as she'd told them to, they stopped in front of the trees. The four Parkway Girls thundered in after them. "I thought I warned you not to run!" snarled Tanya.

"*Get 'em!*" squawked Bella.

Then Lily stepped out from behind her tree.

Chapter 14
Victory

As soon as Lily moved, the three trees came to life. The crows shifted, cawed, and spread their wings. They were waiting for the next batch of food. The Parkway Girls looked up and groaned in horror. The colour drained from their faces like water running out of a sink. "Oh, holy shit!" Tanya croaked.

"Something *wrong*, Tanya?" doll-smiled Lily.

The Morrigan left its branch and flapped to the ground.

"Don't do this!" moaned Jade. Her knees looked as if they might give way. She was terrified.

"*Please!*" begged Jenny.

There was a silence, broken only by cawing and the weird sound of claws and feathers moving against branches.

"I'll give you one last chance," hissed Lily, in her most evil voice. "Leave these girls alone. Leave *everyone* alone. Or I'll find you, OK?" She took a step forward and the crows, expecting goodies, started to move around and croak loudly, as if they were just about to attack. "I'll find you and call them and ... they'll come!"

Then, as if it understood, the Morrigan lifted its terrifying beak and began to stalk towards the Parkway Girls. The Girls inched backwards, their faces like white masks of fear. They didn't turn around until they reached the mouth of the alley. Then they turned. And they *ran*.

"Anna? Bryony?" whispered Lily.

"Yes?" squeaked Anna.

"You go now. Just walk out slowly. You'll be fine. I'll see you tomorrow, OK?"

"Thank you, Crow Girl!" sobbed Anna. Bryony didn't move. She looked as if she'd been turned to stone. Anna took her hand and, not looking back, pulled her out of the alley.

Lily waited for a count of five. Then a huge grin split her face, and she darted back for the food bag. She grabbed a great fistful of scraps and threw them up into the air. The crows went mad, flapping and circling, catching bits of bacon rind and cake and cheese. Lily danced into the alley, and the crows followed her in a black, croaking cloud. On the road, she calmed down. She thought maybe Anna and Bryony were looking back at her, and further off she could see the Parkway Girls, huddled in a group, looking back too.

Lily drew herself up tall, and walked off towards the Wakeless Woods. She went on throwing scraps into the air, and the crows went on flying round her head. It was a terrific show.

Suddenly she heard someone hammering at an upstairs window of one of the houses at the top of the lane. She looked up. It was Kyle, with Marsha and a couple of other friends. They were all crowded together and looking out. They waved and shouted, and she gave the thumbs up sign. Kyle yelled that he'd see her at his house in 20 minutes' time.

Lily blew him a kiss, then she carried on. She led her crows back to the woods in a victory parade.

Chapter 15
Christmas

Kyle had arranged to meet Lily at four o'clock on Christmas afternoon at the gate at the bottom of his garden. Lily was going to feed the crows, then come back to Kyle's house later.

"Hey!" she called, as she spotted him waiting. "Merry Christmas!"

"Merry Christmas to you, gorgeous!" he called back.

Lily was wearing her new coat with a bold, scarlet scarf. Kyle thought she looked even more fantastic than usual. They kissed and hugged each other, then they kissed again, a lot slower. Then, at last, Lily drew back and handed Kyle a slinky carrier bag. "Here's your present," she said. "It's wrapped up but don't even *look* in the bag till I get back."

"I wouldn't dare. You're far too scary."

"This is true. Have you got your offerings?"

"Yes," he grinned. He nodded towards a full and lumpy plastic bag by the hedge.

"Blimey, that's loads!" Lily laughed.

"Well, there's lots of turkey skin. Hey! If they eat another bird does it make them cannibals?"

"Don't think they'll care. What else?"

"Mashed up mince pie – "

"They *love* pastry!"

"And a load of ham fat."

"Kyle, you're a star! They're gonna have a real Christmas feast. I've got some cheese, and broken biscuits …"

"Paper hats? Crackers?"

"Don't take the piss!"

"I wasn't." He put his arms round her again.

"Come with me," she murmured.

"No way."

"They'd never attack you if you've got all that food ..."

"Lily – we've talked about this! I don't trust them. They want me out of the way. They're jealous of me!"

Lily laughed, then kissed him again.

"Now go," he said. "And don't be too long. There's a lovely open fire in our back room, and no one's there."

"Really?"

"They're all watching some boring film. We can have it *all* to ourselves."

"Fantastic," said Lily. "OK, I'm off." They kissed again. "Bye!" And kissed again. "I'm *really* going now, OK?" She picked up the bag he'd left by the hedge, and set off into the woods.

"I'll be waiting!" he called out.

If Lily could have seen the way he watched her as she walked away into the trees, the way he stood there until he couldn't see her any more ... If she could have seen how everything in him was longing for her, she might have turned right round again, and walked back into his arms.

But then again, she might not.

Kraaaw! Kraaaaw!

Kraaaaaaaaw!